STAR WARS

FORCES OF DESTINY™

STAR WARS

FORCES OF DESTINY™

Daring Adventures:

Volume II

Written by
Emma Carlson Berne

DISNEY

LUCASFILM
PRESS

Los Angeles • New York

First Edition, October 2017
1 3 5 7 9 10 8 6 4 2
FAC-029261-17230
Library of Congress Control Number on file
ISBN 978-1-368-01120-4

Visit the official *Star Wars* website at: www.starwars.com.

SUSTAINABLE
FORESTRY
INITIATIVE
Certified Sourcing
www.sfiprogram.org
SFI-01415

CONTENTS

AHSOKA
The Padawan Path

A MESSAGE FROM MAZ:

You are listening, my young friend? I am glad
you have come to see me, Maz Kanata, by
my fire here in the forest. The forest is home
to many creatures that like the velvety dark
night and the friendly crackle of a fire, like me.
And that like stories—like you. Many, many
wanderers across the years have come to me
for help. I do help them—why would I not, when
I have lived for so long? And I will help you,
too, friend. But you must listen carefully.

What's that I hear, croaking nearby? Ah,
it is a flurrg. Come here, little friend! And

another one of you, too! Word travels fast among you flurrgs. Come closer to the fire, Flurrg Two. My, these stories are getting popular. Of course, there are as many stories about heroes as there are stars in the sky. Gather round now. I'll tell you of heroes who never let a problem stop them, no matter the size or the shape. And remember, the choices we make, the actions we take, the moments— both big and small—shape us into forces of destiny.

CHAPTER 1

Ahsoka Tano ran through the streets of Coruscant, a planet that was one big city.

Above her towered the thousands of skyscrapers in which the wealthy watched over the city from their high perches and breathed their own supply of clean air.

Levels below her was the massive

underworld in which the poor and criminal lived in filth, the air filled with toxic fumes from the Coruscant factories. But that day, on the middle level of the planet, sun filtered its hazy way onto the streets, speeders whirred past, children ran by laughing and playing, and Ahsoka Tano was late.

When you're a new Padawan and your master and Master Yoda are waiting for you at the Jedi Temple, and when you're a Padawan who has been told too many times to count that you have a long way to go before achieving Jedi Knight status—well, it's just not a good idea to be late.

Ahsoka's comlink crackled on her wrist.

"Ahsoka? You on your way?" Anakin's voice cut through the static.

He hadn't wanted an apprentice at first—he'd made that abundantly clear—and she hadn't particularly wanted to be his. But their relationship had shifted. She and Anakin were good together as Padawan and master. Ahsoka had been working hard. She felt a sort of peace settle in her as she continued to develop the Force. She'd learned how to focus and calm her mind.

Her comlink crackled again and Ahsoka raised her wrist to her mouth.

"I'm on my way, Master! I just finished patrol."

She could tell Anakin was tense; he didn't want Master Yoda to be kept waiting.

"Well, get back here, and hurry! I'm waiting for you."

The comlink went silent. Ahsoka winced and ran a little faster. She just had to make it to the Jedi Temple, which she glimpsed in the distance. She could see its five white spires rising high into the hazy afternoon sky.

CHAPTER 2

Anakin Skywalker tapped his foot on the white stone floor of the Jedi Temple courtyard. The sound echoed. Yoda, standing quietly in front of the Great Tree, looked over at Anakin.

Anakin stopped tapping. He paced over to the ancient Jedi Master. The thought suddenly flashed through his mind that the gnarled and twisted trunk of the Force-sensitive tree was like Yoda's gnarled and bent body. Both were as old as the ages; both had seen more than he ever would.

"Master Yoda!" Anakin bent his head in respect.

"Ahsoka will be here soon. I know this ceremony is very important to her."

The last part he was sure of. He just wished he could be as sure of the first part. He struggled to stop the doubt and irritation that twisted suddenly inside him. He'd been so sure Ahsoka was ready for the ceremony to receive her Padawan beads. But the tardiness—was he wrong? Lateness was a sign of selfishness—not a characteristic of a Jedi Knight.

Yoda's raspy voice broke through Anakin's thoughts.

"Deserved your Padawan is of this honor, young Skywalker."

Anakin looked at his master, surprised. Once again, Yoda knew what he was thinking. Now if only he could be sure the old Jedi Master was right.

CHAPTER 3

Ahsoka was beginning to pant as her booted feet pounded through the streets. The sun was strong overhead. She wiped a trickle of sweat from the side of her face. It wasn't so bad, she told herself. She was only a few minutes late.

"No! Oh, no!" A voice came from somewhere nearby.

Automatically, Ahsoka slowed and listened.

The buzz of speeders, chattering of shoppers, clanging of metal from some workers on a building behind her. Maybe someone had just dropped something. She picked up the pace again.

But she'd only gone three more steps when the scream came again.

"Nooo! Get away! Someone help!"

There was a crash and more screaming. Ahsoka skidded to a halt, listening hard. The commotion was coming from one block over. She sighed and looked north. The Temple spires were so close.

Ahsoka clenched her hands, then turned and ran toward the screaming.

She darted across the street, dodging

speeders, and dashed over to the next block. She was almost driven back by a flood of people running the opposite way.

"Get back!" someone shouted. "It's gone crazy!"

What's gone crazy? Ahsoka wondered as she ran past a row of offices.

She soon had her answer. In front of a clothing shop, an industrial cleaning droid was malfunctioning—badly. It spun wildly, crashing randomly into waste bins and light poles. The street was so crowded, the people nearest the droid were trapped against each other, with everyone struggling to escape. Ahsoka skidded to a halt with the screams of the crowd flooding her head. She looked around for a

Coruscant police officer, but there was none. This one was going to be all her.

The droid let out a series of earsplitting beeps and suddenly charged into the crowd. It was going for something—then the crowd parted and Ahsoka saw a fishlike Aleena woman crouched against the wall of the clothing shop, clutching a similarly fishy-looking toddler in her arms. The droid was heading right toward them, swinging wildly with its outstretched claw arms. She could see they were trapped by a wall on one side and a stack of heavy crates on the other.

Ahsoka stretched out her arm, fingers wide, and focused her mind deeply, calmly, completely. She bored into the droid with her eyes, feeling the Force welling from her mind, flowing down her arm, and bursting out through her palm—straight toward the droid.

The droid flew backward suddenly from the Force push, away from the mother and baby, but its long metal arm whirred, rotating its claws like whirling blades and barely missing the faces of some of the people in the crowd. Ahsoka sucked in a breath. A blow from one of those arms would do some serious damage.

Ahsoka leapt forward, but before she could do any more, the droid smashed into the wall of the shop. It tilted from the impact of the blow, spun, and zoomed straight toward Ahsoka as if from a slingshot. Its arms clanged against a metal pipe that ran at shoulder level along the street, and slimy water sprayed Ahsoka from top to bottom.

"Aaghh!" She yelled as the foul odor of the water rose around her. She swiped the slime from her face with her forearm. The dirty water was pouring from the pipe and pooling in the street.

"Get out of here!" she yelled at the crowd.

People scattered. The mother tried to drag her child away, but the droid turned and blocked her way every time she moved.

The droid's whir rose to a scream. It had spotted Ahsoka and was speeding straight for her. Ahsoka looked around wildly—there! A trash crate stood just to her left. Ahsoka jumped in and dropped to the floor of the crate, which sat just above the smelly, pooling water. The droid crashed into the outside of the crate, shaking it. People gasped. Ahsoka glanced up. Faces stared down at her from the top of one of the buildings, where the crowd had gathered.

The droid backed away and then rolled forward and smashed the crate again. Not much time left.

CHAPTER 4

A bird tweeted softly in the corner of the Temple courtyard. A breeze stirred the leaves of the Great Tree. Yoda stood beside Anakin in the shade of the branches, his hands folded over the top of his stick. He cleared his throat. Anakin jumped at the sound.

Yoda placed a wrinkled hand on Anakin's sleeve.

"Relax, you must," he said.

Anakin nodded and unclenched his jaw.

"Don't worry. She'll be here."

He wasn't sure if he was talking to Yoda or himself.

Yoda nodded. "Know this, I do."

Anakin forced a smile. This was all a mistake. She wasn't ready. She wasn't ready! And now he was going to embarrass himself in front of Master Yoda, the greatest Jedi Master ever to have lived. How could Ahsoka let him down like this? He'd been so sure this was the right moment for her to receive her Padawan beads.

CHAPTER 5

From inside the crate, Ahsoka considered her options. She couldn't risk an extended fight with the droid. There were too many civilians around. Someone was bound to get hurt. Whatever she did, it would have to be fast.

The crate shook as the droid slammed into it again. Ahsoka peeked out. She noticed that the droid seemed to be short-circuiting, wisps of smoke coming from its controls. Her eyes drifted up to see a dripping water pipe overhead. She grinned. It was time to see what some water could do. Ahsoka bent her knees, braced herself, and pulled out her lightsaber. With a flick of her thumb, she activated it.

The droid whizzed backward, through a big puddle just in front of the crate. Ahsoka waited. Every part of her concentrated, gathering her strength. The droid paused on its backward pass, gearing up to go forward again.

The droid zoomed ahead. Just as it went under the dripping water pipe, Ahsoka leapt high out of the crate, jumped onto the droid, and used it as a boost to slice through the pipe with her lightsaber. Water soaked the droid, which immediately started to spark and fizzle. Ahsoka leapt off and landed safely on the ground.

The droid continued to break down in a spectacular fashion. White lights popped with a terrific bang and a loud crackling. The crowd above screamed and covered their ears. The droid spun around and around, first fast, then slower and slower, until gradually it turned on its base one more time, then with a low whine dropped face-first into the large puddle of water and went still.

The watching crowd burst into applause.

Ahsoka let out a long breath. Her knees were a little shaky.

The Aleena woman ran up to Ahsoka, clutching her child close.

"Thank you for saving us!"

The woman threw one arm around Ahsoka.

"Who are you?"

Ahsoka patted the woman on the back. "That's not important. What's important is, are you all right?"

The woman nodded. Ahsoka looked into the child's dirty, tearstained face.

"And are *you* all right?"

The child looked at Ahsoka with huge, solemn eyes, then opened her mouth wide to reveal a blue piece of candy on her tongue.

Ahsoka laughed.

"I guess that answers my question."

Then the spires of the Temple, visible over the buildings, caught her eye.

"The ceremony!" she gasped.

CHAPTER 6

Thirty minutes. She was thirty minutes late!

Anakin groaned inwardly. He glanced at Yoda for what felt like the hundredth time. The Jedi stood quietly under the tree, hands folded. The sun was almost directly overhead and the stone of the Temple floor was growing hot.

Anakin shifted as the warmth seeped through the leather soles of his boots. This was a mistake. She wasn't ready—clearly! They should just leave. He had opened his mouth to tell Yoda that when Yoda spoke.

"Have faith in her, you must," he said calmly.

Anakin bit the words back.

"I do," he said instead.

Or I did, he thought.

Suddenly, the sound of light running feet echoed in the outer courtyard.

"Sorry I'm late," Ahsoka panted.

CHAPTER 7

Ahsoka skidded to a stop in the inner courtyard. Squinting against the sun in her eyes, she could make out Anakin standing under the Great Tree. He looked tense. Ahsoka could only guess how long he'd been waiting for her.

"Ahsoka! What happened?" Anakin asked. He stepped forward, his brows knitting together.

Ahsoka glanced down at herself—green

muck splattered her dress, legs, and boots. She took a deep breath, opened her mouth . . . then closed it. She was already late. Best to keep this short.

"Let's just say . . . there were some complications."

She bowed her head. If the Padawan beads were coming her way, then they were. They symbolized her advancement in her study to become a Jedi Knight. If her lateness had cost her that, then it was already decided. There was nothing she could do at this point.

She stared at her soaked boots. The heat from the stone floor crept through the soles. Then she saw a shadow—a small, short shadow—moving toward her. The shadow had big ears.

She looked up.

Yoda was standing in front of her, holding something in his closed fist.

"Humble and brave, you are. A sign of maturity this is. . . ."

Ahsoka exhaled. She heard Anakin let out his breath at the same time. She watched Master Yoda. A huge grin spread across his face. Lightness flooded through Ahsoka.

Yoda stepped close to Ahsoka and she knelt in front of him. He held his hand over her head and spoke firmly.

"Outstanding growth you have shown, Ahsoka Tano. On the path to becoming a Jedi Knight, you are."

Ahsoka's throat swelled as she thrilled at his words. She looked up at Anakin. *Thank you,* she mouthed. He had trained her right. At last, they both knew it.

Yoda opened his closed hand. Padawan beads cascaded down from it, glittering in the sun. Ahsoka rose and accepted the beads. She bowed her head.

"Thank you, Master Yoda."

She removed the jewelry string she always wore on her montrals and clipped the new Padawan beads to the end. Carefully, she replaced the string. She could feel the added weight immediately. It felt good—very good.

Anakin stepped up to her. His wide blue eyes were twinkling. "I'm proud of you, Snips."

"Thank you, Master," Ahsoka answered. And out of the corner of her eye, she saw Yoda still smiling, proud of them both.

LEIA
BEASTS OF ECHO BASE

A MeSSaGe FROM MaZ:

The fire feels nice, doesn't it? Look at the
embers flying into the sky. They look like stars,
don't they? Isn't that right, my flurrg friends?
I'm glad you're still here, listening. Now, what
was I saying? Oh, yes. There's more than one
way to solve a problem.

What's that, little flurrg? I hear your croak.
Say it again, so I can understand. Oh! That's
very true. Lean close, my friend. As our flurrg
says, you don't always have to *be* big to *think*
big.

CHAPTER 8

Princess Leia Organa stood in the middle of the main hangar deck on Echo Base, pilots and workers scurrying around her as they went about their assigned tasks. She shivered and wondered if she would ever get used to how cold Hoth was. She even felt cold in her dreams at night.

The cold is part of what makes this such

a good hiding place for the Rebellion, she

reminded herself. *Focus on what's important!*

She looked down at the plans on the

datapad she was holding. The base was nearly

ready. They just needed to complete some

of the underground storage chambers and

corridors, then stock them. She'd given orders

for work on the corridors early that morning.

Chewbacca had volunteered to do some of the

digging, which she appreciated. His Wookiee

strength would be a big help.

"Princess Leia!"

She looked up to see General Rieekan, the

leader of the base, approaching.

"I'm glad I found you," he said. "I wanted

to go over a few last-minute changes to our

defense strategy in case of attack."

"Of course, General," Leia said. "Let's go to the command center."

She shivered. "It's usually a little bit warmer in there."

General Rieekan grinned in agreement and turned with Leia to walk toward the command center. They were about halfway there when Leia spotted her friend Luke Skywalker on one side of the hangar.

"Leia!" Luke called.

He was crouched by the landing gear of a snowspeeder, welding something into place.

"Have you seen Chewie? I need his help with this and he said he'd be here to give me a hand over two hours ago."

"He volunteered to help with digging tunnels this morning, but he should have been finished by now," Leia said. "Did you say he was two *hours* late?"

Luke straightened up from his work, his eyes darkening with worry.

"Yes, two hours. And he's never late."

"No, he's not." Leia's brow creased.

Rieekan looked from her to Luke. She could tell Luke was thinking the same thing she was: for Chewie to be so late, something had to be wrong.

"I'll go find him," Leia announced.

"I'll come with you," Luke said.

"No, stay here in case Chewie shows up. I'll take Artoo with me." Both Luke and the general seemed hesitant. "We'll be *fine*," she assured them. "Artoo and I can take care of ourselves."

CHAPTER 9

Leia strode quickly down the icy corridor. You had to move fast on Hoth—otherwise you'd turn into an icicle.

She had to find Chewie. Leia held her lantern high. The light illuminated the tunnel of packed snow and ice with pipes and wires strung on both sides. The upstairs corridors were bustling with personnel, but not many people went down to that remote area, still being built.

Leia looked at R2-D2, blinking by her side. The droid was always ready for action and had whistled happily when she'd asked him to help her find Chewbacca.

"I hope Chewie's okay," she said, with a hint of worry in her voice.

The Wookiee was very strong and a great pilot, and plenty of other things that were helpful to the Rebellion, but most important, he was a loyal friend, and Leia couldn't bear the thought of anything bad happening to him.

R2-D2 beeped optimistically in response, and Leia smiled.

Leia looked around. All she could see were some metal door parts, thrown all over the floor as if someone had abandoned installing them, and a driller the crews must have left down there. A little snake of anxiety began wriggling in Leia's stomach.

Her boots scraped softly on the ice as she and R2-D2 crept to the end of the corridor. Leia had no idea what was at the end of the hallway.

The floor sloped gradually downward into complete darkness. Leia paused and raised her lantern high. The yellow light did little to penetrate the murk.

"Chewie!" she called.

Her voice echoed back at her, *Chewie-ewie-ewie*... Her ears strained for a returning roar from the Wookiee. But there was only the eerie darkness, the heavy silence.

R2-D2 rolled up, and Leia rested her hand on his smooth dome. A gentle warmth came from his motor and his bright blinking lights.

"Chewbacca!" she shouted again.

This time, Leia heard a faint roar from the depths of the corridor. It was coming from beyond the slope. Leia's heart leapt. Chewie wasn't lost! He was down there—somewhere. But there must be a reason he wasn't coming up to them—and she was going to find out what it was.

"That sure sounds like Chewie. Come on, Artoo!"

R2-D2 whirred behind her as she led the way down the slick slope. The lantern burned steadily, lighting the way a few meters in front of them. The slope flattened out. Leia could tell they were in some kind of a cavern— one she hadn't even known existed. Chewie must have discovered the cavern while he was digging the corridor. How big it was, she couldn't tell, even as she swung the lantern left and right. It *must* have been where Chewie howled from, but she couldn't see him.

The little astromech droid beeped at her.

"We're going to find him, don't worry. I've

got this." Leia stepped forward. "Chewie? Are you here?"

Suddenly, her swinging light caught the Wookiee, crouched in a corner.

"Chewie! Is that you? Why didn't you say anything?"

Chewie growled very softly. His face was twisted with tension and he didn't rise from his crouch.

"What? What's wrong?"

Leia knelt beside him. He was squatting next to a large pile of snow.

"Come on out, Chewie, everything's all right! It's so cold down here. Let's go back—I brought a lantern, see?"

Chewie shook his head violently, strands of

fur catching the light. He gestured toward the snow mound. Leia looked at it more closely.

It was breathing.

Leia realized that what she thought was a pile of snow was actually a wampa—one of the fur-covered snow beasts that lived on Hoth.

Leia's pulse thudded in her ears. She hadn't brought her blaster. She hadn't brought anything besides a droid and a lantern. Okay, so no weapons. They weren't going to be able to fight the creature. Not even Chewie, a big strong Wookiee, could fight a wampa. So the most important thing would be to sneak away without waking it.

"Okay, Chewie," she whispered. "Very slowly, let's go—"

The wampa stirred and, reaching out with its long-clawed paws, pulled Chewie against it like a stuffed toy. Next to the giant wampa, Chewie looked very small. Eyes still closed, the wampa nuzzled the Wookiee happily. Chewie's blue eyes stared out from the mix of white and brown fur like two huge marbles. He let out a low, worried moan.

R2-D2 beeped softly.

"It does look dangerous, Artoo," Leia whispered back. "But Chewie's coming with us. I'm just trying to think of how to rescue him."

Suddenly, a loud crackle broke the quiet. Leia's comlink blinked on and C-3PO's voice filled the cavern.

"Princess? Princess Leia? Are you there? Master Luke is wondering if you've found Chewbacca."

Leia grabbed her comlink from her belt. *"Threepio,"* she whispered. *"SHHH!"*

"I'm so sorry. You're breaking up," Threepio crackled. "There appears to be a lot of static—"

Frantically, Leia thumbed the *off* button, but it was too late. The beast began to stir, like a mound of shifting snow. Chewie scrambled away as it swiped at him. For an instant, Leia stared up into gaping jaws below a slimy snout. The wampa reared up to its full height and lifted its head. It let out a full-throated roar that boomed around the cavern.

"Go, go!" Leia pushed R2-D2 in front of her toward the exit as Chewie whirled around and sped after them.

The wampa roared again. Its shadow loomed dark on the white wall. Its mouth opened wide and saliva dripped from its yellow fangs. It ran toward them with frightening speed.

"It's gaining on us!" Leia shouted, panting up the ice-covered slope. "Get going!"

R2-D2 buzzed up the slope slowly. He was having trouble moving on the slick surface. Chewie dug his long black claws into the ground and pushed the droid.

Leia tried to grip with her feet, but her boots weren't much help on the ice. The slope was like a slide—sending them right back toward the wampa. She shot a glance over her shoulder. The wampa ran easily toward them, its long claws digging into the ice like it was climbing a ladder. Its big black eyes were fixed on them. The rank odor of its fur filled the air.

"We can't let it get into the base!" Leia shouted.

Her voice shook. Her heart pounded so hard in her ears she could barely hear her own words.

"Chewie, run ahead and seal that passageway! I'll distract it!"

Chewie roared in response and picked up R2-D2. Carrying the droid like a package, he sprinted up the slope toward the hallway.

Leia spun around, her breath whistling in her ears. She had to keep the wampa near her, without letting it get *too* near. It didn't seem very smart. Maybe she could distract it. Perhaps it liked heat and light. And she *had* heat and light—the lantern.

"Here, boy!" she called softly. She swung the lantern gently.

The wampa slowed at the sound of her voice and stood several meters away, facing her. It roared and Leia almost lost her nerve. She gritted her teeth. She had to give Chewie and R2-D2 at least a few moments to get the door built to seal the passageway. They'd have it done in no time ... she hoped!

The wampa's head swung as it followed the lantern. It made a snuffling noise that Leia hoped meant it was happy. It padded toward her. The odor of its fur and breath grew stronger—rank and thick. Its tongue hung to one side, dripping thick blobs of saliva onto the ice, where they froze immediately.

Leia kept her eyes fixed on the beast's face,
willing it to come forward. "Come on, boy,"
she whispered.

"Easy. Easy."

CHAPTER 10

Chewie and R2-D2 worked frantically to install the door so they could keep the wampa from entering the base. Chewie turned the drill up to top speed and roared at R2-D2, who was quickly screwing in bolt after bolt. R2-D2's whirrs rose to a high-pitched whine. He snatched up another bolt and screwed it into the hole so fast it looked like a blur of gray metal. A little curl of smoke rose from each bolt hole.

Chewie threw down the drill and raised the side of the door frame, struggling with the awkward slab of metal. R2-D2 spun around and shot bolts into the slab, one after the other.

Chewie leapt up and grabbed the welding torch. Almost done.

CHAPTER 11

Leia's eyes felt pasted open. Sweat trickled down the side of her neck and into her uniform. The wampa seemed hypnotized by the gently swaying lantern. That was good. But just how long would the trance last? That was the question.

"Come on," she muttered.

In her head, Leia willed Chewie and R2-D2 to finish their job faster. She didn't know how much longer she could hold off the creature.

The wampa suddenly shook its head and roared. The sound blasted Leia's ears.

And there's my answer.

The wampa had grown tired of the swaying light, apparently. Now it wanted more interesting fare—like a rebel princess. Leia flattened herself against the side of the tunnel. The wampa charged.

Leia sprang out in front of the beast, holding the lantern high. She'd only have one chance. When she was sure the wampa was focused on the lantern, she flung it away, back down the slope toward the cavern.

The wampa skidded to a halt, following the

arc of the tiny light as it bounced down the icy slope. Leia stood frozen. Then, with a roar, the wampa turned and ran after the lantern.

No sense in waiting around!

Leia ran back up the slope toward Chewie and R2-D2. In about five seconds, the wampa would discover the lantern *wasn't* a tasty dinner—that in fact, something that *would* make a tasty dinner was running away—and it would be back.

She grabbed her comlink from her belt and flicked it on as she ran.

"Chewie! How's that door coming?"

She heard Chewie roaring and R2-D2 beeping through the comm.

"I'm almost there!" Leia shouted. "Stop arguing and finish!"

She snapped the comlink back onto her belt just as an angry bellow came from behind her.

"And . . . he's coming for his dinner," Leia muttered to herself.

The wampa roared again. Closer this time. Leia picked up the pace and threw a glance back. It was closer than ever, running along the icy floor at an amazing speed.

She could see the door ahead. It was open, but Chewie stood in front of it, trying to weld something on with a torch. R2-D2 was drilling at the bottom.

"Here we come!" Leia shouted to them.

The wampa was only a meter or so behind her now. Leia could smell the musk of its fur. Her throat ached and her lungs screamed for rest.

The door was just ahead. The wampa swiped at her back, narrowly missing. Leia flung herself forward right as Chewie leapt to the side. She dove through the opening.

"Now, Chewie!"

Chewie hit the activation button. The door hissed closed. The wampa slammed against the other side. For a moment, Leia, Chewie, and R2-D2 stood there, listening to the wampa throwing itself against the door in rage.

Bang! Bang! Bang!

A dent appeared in the metal. Leia held her breath as Chewie squeezed her hand. Then, slowly, the bangs grew weaker. The wampa was getting tired. At last there was silence. Leia held her finger up to the other two and tiptoed to the door. She laid her ear against the metal just in time to hear the *scritch-scritch* of the wampa's claws on the ice as it padded away down the tunnel.

Roaring joyfully, Chewie flung his arms around Leia and picked her up in a Wookiee hug. Leia hugged him back.

"You're welcome, Chewie. But I should say thank you to you, too. And Artoo. Without your fancy tool work, I'd be that wampa's dinner for sure."

Chewie set Leia down, and R2-D2 beeped happily. The three friends left the dark tunnel behind and headed back to their busy life on Echo Base.

JYN
THE STRANGER

A Message from Maz:

We've been telling tales a long time tonight, haven't we? My throat is a bit dry. But see? I have some broth, here, in this pot. And two bowls—one for you and one for me. Hot. And savory, too! It warms the soul. Ah, the flurrgs are coming to us now. Look at this one. He's brought his family, too.

What is that flurrg saying? Hungry, are

you, my friend? Soup? This is what you want?
Well, here. I can't eat while you go hungry.
Open your mouth. I'll pour it in. And some for
your family, too—here, all of you.

But back to our stories. At this point you
may be asking, "What makes a hero?" The
answer may not be as complicated as you
think.

CHAPTER 12

At midday in the Garel City marketplace, vendors wrapped in robes shouted their wares, selling fruit and sausages, pans, navigators and comlinks, tools, and lengths of cloth.

Artisans crouched over low tables, whacking at metal rings or feeding fabric through sewing machines. Politicians in long garments walked and talked together, rough-looking smugglers eyed everyone suspiciously, and groups of stormtroopers in shiny white armor stood at every corner, blasters resting on their forearms. Children ran, shouting and weaving through people's legs, while shoppers of different species fingered cloth and squeezed produce, arguing with the vendors.

Jyn Erso wandered through the section of fruit vendors. She kept her body relaxed through long practice, but her eyes darted around her. Her jaw was clenched, and her hands tucked into her pockets were balled into fists.

She had to keep on the lookout. If the

stormtroopers caught her, they'd surely lock her up. She had gotten into too much trouble with the Empire.

Feeling a fruit at one vendor's stall, Jyn gritted her teeth against the sick feeling that always rose when she thought of the past few years.

Everyone she'd ever loved or trusted was gone—her father, her mother. Saw Gerrera, the rebel who had taken her in, had abandoned her long before.

She'd been doing her best ever since to survive on her own and keep from starving. Sometimes she had to do things she wasn't proud of.

Like now.

Her contact had promised her the man she was meeting would pay a lot of credits for what Jyn had. And he'd better. She'd spent weeks forging valuable documents for him. Forgery was one of the skills she'd had to develop to survive. If the man gave her enough credits, she could disappear again for a while. Jyn looked around. Where was he? By the meiloorun fruit stall, that's what she'd told him.

What if it's a setup? she thought suddenly, and her stomach plunged.

She felt sweat break out on her forehead. Someone might have offered him a better price to inform on her. Jyn resisted the impulse to flee.

"There you are," someone with a gruff voice

said in her ear, and Jyn jumped, bumping the man who had appeared at her side.

He was draped in black robes, with a fold of the cloth over his head. She couldn't see his face. She didn't like it when she couldn't see people's faces.

"You got the credits?" she said. "I have to get out of here."

"What's the hurry?" The grating voice seemed to come from a long way under the robes.

The sick feeling in Jyn's stomach got worse.

"I have the documents, if that's what you're worried about."

Jyn glanced around again. No one seemed to be listening. The fruit vendor was filling a woman's basket with fat orange meilooruns. Jyn pulled out the datacube that contained the documents. She held it up, then pulled it back fast when the man's hand shot out.

"Hang on, friend. The credits first."

"The datacube first, *friend*," the man said. "Or I'm out of here and you're left with nothing."

Jyn thought about it, but she didn't have much of a choice. She shook her head.

"All right, quick."

She slapped the datacube into his cloth-wrapped hand.

"Now the credits."

She hoped he wouldn't try to cheat her. She didn't want to get into a fight. What good would it do anyway, in a crowded place like that?

The man put his hand into his robes and pulled out a bundle of credits wrapped in burlap.

"They're all there. Ten thousand. Just like we agreed."

Jyn exhaled slowly as she took the packet. The man nodded at her and melted back into the crowd as quietly as he had come. Jyn unfolded the bundle and counted the credits. Ten thousand. Her knees were shaky with relief. She was fine now, she told herself. Everything was fine. She folded the burlap again carefully and tucked the bundle beneath her shirt.

Her heart lighter than it had been for a long time, Jyn dug a stray credit out of her pocket.

"This one," Jyn told the elderly fruit vendor, plucking a soft orange meiloorun from the pile.

He nodded at her, and she tossed the fruit into the air a few times before catching it and taking a juicy, dripping bite.

"There she is!"

A deep filtered voice came from behind her, and Jyn turned. A group of four stormtroopers was clustered around a little girl who had

backed into a pile of teakettles. The little girl wore a torn dress, her face grubby with dirt, her hair tangled and uncared for. She clutched a tooka cat in her arms.

"Please! Leave me alone!" she cried, cowering against the pile of kettles, holding the tooka cat to her chest.

A crowd gathered to watch. The stormtroopers loomed over the girl, their white-and-black armor blinding in the sunlight.

"You are in violation of code three-one-zero. Hand over the animal," one of them said, his filtered voice loud even amid the din of the market.

CHAPTER 13

Jyn squeezed the fruit she held. Of course they'd go after a little girl with a pet. They didn't have anything better to do. And they preferred to prey on the weak. She'd seen it many times. Bile rose in her throat and almost choked her as she watched the stormtroopers loom over the girl.

"She's all I have," the girl pleaded. Tears streaked her dirty face.

"Too bad," another trooper replied. He reached down and grabbed the tooka cat by the scruff of its neck. The creature screeched and the little girl wailed.

"Please! Please!" she cried, reaching out toward the animal.

No one in the crowd made a move to help her.

"Give her back!"

The girl stumbled against the pyramid of teakettles, knocking them over with a clatter.

Rage boiled up in Jyn, and suddenly, without thinking, she pitched the meiloorun at the stormtrooper holding the cat. The fruit splattered orange against his pristine white helmet. A gasp rose from the crowd. The trooper wheeled around.

"Who threw that?"

Jyn stood up straight, eyes boring into his blank mask of a face.

"I did," she snarled. "And I suggest you pick on someone your own size."

A tiny voice deep inside her told her—again—to step away.

Mind your own business. Keep your head down. Look out for yourself and no one else.

But she couldn't stop. Something about the little girl's tangled hair, her smudged face . . . She was alone. That much was clear. Jyn knew what that felt like—to be small and alone in the world.

The troopers ran toward Jyn, their footsteps pounding the hard-packed earth. Jyn tensed, waiting. The fruit-splattered trooper grabbed for her. Just as he leaned forward, she launched herself at him, kicking him hard in the gut.

"There you go!" she shouted.

The force of the kick sent him stumbling backward into the trooper behind him. They went down in a tangle of white-plated arms and legs, smashing into the counter of a stall selling bolts of fabric and bringing piles of striped cloth tumbling down around them.

The crowd scattered, sensing big trouble. Jyn flashed an *okay* sign to the little girl and without waiting for the troopers to heave themselves up, slid behind the sparkly silk of a merchant's tent.

"No, not here!" the merchant said with alarm, looking up from his workbench.

"I don't want any trouble in here—you take your fight somewhere else, girl."

Jyn barely heard him.

"Just for a minute," she panted, flattening herself against the silken wall and peering around the flap.

The two other troopers ran toward the tent. One still clutched the terrified tooka cat by the neck. The animal's desperate yowls were almost lost in the sound of the troopers' heavy footsteps.

Jyn grabbed a pole leaning against the

tent and waited, tense. Her breath whistled in her ears. The red-and-yellow silk of the tent wall in front of her glowed like sunlight and the sounds of the market disappeared until she could hear only her own breath and the footsteps of the troopers, feel only her sweaty hands on the pole and the thud of her pulse in her palms.

The troopers ran toward the tent entrance. Jyn knelt and quickly thrust the pole out at knee level. Both troopers hit it at the same time, flipping forward onto their faces. They grunted and dust flew from the ground. The cat leapt free and took off through the market.

Jyn dropped the pole with a clatter and stepped out from behind the tent flap.

"And you're welcome!" she shouted at the troopers, who were scrambling to their feet.

"Grab her!" one yelled.

Jyn sprinted off in the direction the cat had run. Shoppers dodged out of her way as she glimpsed the tip of its purple tail, then lost it as it disappeared under a sausage vendor's grill.

The glowing coals of the hanging grill gave Jyn an idea. She shot a quick glance over her shoulder. The troopers weren't far behind. Panting, Jyn scrambled atop a nearby metal barrel and—ignoring the shouts as the troopers spotted her—leapt behind the grill. The vendor stared at her wide-eyed, a long-handled fork topped with sausage in his hand.

"Hello," Jyn told him. "Sorry about all this."

The shouts of the troopers were close now. Jyn scanned the stall fast. There! A rubber hose attached to the stall's water pipe. Jyn grabbed the hose and tried to turn the tap handle. Stuck! The thing was stuck!

Come on, come on!

The troopers were almost on her. The handle would not turn. Suddenly, a squirt of something black splashed onto the handle—oil!

Jyn looked up into the face of the big sausage vendor. A canister of oil dangled from one hand.

"Good luck, girl," he whispered, and backed away as Jyn tried the handle again.

This time it turned!

She cranked the faucet open, then grabbed the hose, aiming it at the grill and spraying water full blast on the hot coals. Steam and smoke billowed out in a great white cloud, surrounding the vendor, the stall, the troopers. Something small and dark yowled and leapt from the steam—the tooka cat!

Jyn wasted no time. She ducked under the grill, flew past the blinded troopers, and darted after the cat, weaving through the stalls and alleyways. The creature ran along a wall above her head. The market was behind them now; the alley was deserted. If only she could catch that cat! As she ran, listening hard for the troopers' heavy footsteps behind her, Jyn cursed herself for landing in another stupid situation. Why did she draw trouble to herself instead of avoiding attention? As if she needed troopers on her tail!

For an instant, she considered giving up, ducking into one of the empty doorways she was flashing past, and getting out of Garel City for a few days, until things calmed down. Then she imagined the little girl's crying face and her heart twisted. She knew a little something about being alone. Jyn clenched her fists and forced her legs to move faster. The tooka cat leapt through an archway at the end of the alley and Jyn flung herself after it, reaching, almost tripping on the metal grates that covered an opening beneath her feet.

Got it!

She snared the animal by a hind leg, then tucked it safely under one arm, wincing as it sunk its teeth into her thumb.

"You should be grateful, my friend," she muttered to the furious animal.

"I don't think those troopers were going to take you anyplace good."

She was at a dead end—boxed in on three sides by buildings. Jyn shot a glance at the archway. Still empty—but she could hear the footsteps now—*thunk, thunk, thunk*—the heavy sound of running boots. The troopers. Jyn backed into a small opening set in the stone wall. It smelled like garbage. The cat meowed and Jyn squeezed its jaws shut with one hand.

Thunk-THUNK thunk-THUNK. The four troopers crowded the archway, blocking the sun.

"Where is she?" one of them asked. It was

the one she'd thrown the fruit at. His helmet was still crusted with dried orange goo. Jyn hoped the cat would keep quiet. She pressed herself farther into the small opening. The troopers looked around.

"She might have gone across the bridge," the tallest one said. "They usually do."

"Yeah," another one agreed. They started to back away from the archway.

Jyn exhaled, accidentally relaxing her grip on the cat's face. As her hand released the pressure on its jaws, the animal let out a long yowl.

"Shhh!" Jyn hissed frantically.

She looked up to see four black-and-white helmets peering down at her.

CHAPTER 14

"Thought you'd hide, did you?" One of the stormtroopers reached for her.

In one movement, Jyn shot through their legs and stuffed the tooka cat down her shirt. The troopers tried to grab her, but they were hampered by the small space. One bumped two others, sending them stumbling against the wall.

Thinking fast, Jyn looked down. The troopers were standing on the metal grate. Jyn yanked her blaster from its holster. Ignoring the thrashing cat inside her shirt, Jyn fired at the grate catches. The catches broke and all four troopers dropped through the opening, grunting and yelling.

Clutching the cat in her shirt, Jyn slid the blaster back into its holster and sprinted through the archway, leaving the troopers struggling to climb out of the hole.

Jyn ran down the deserted alleyway and hooked a sharp right back into the marketplace. Only then, surrounded by the bustle of the crowd, did she stop, lean against a wall, and take a deep breath. She wiped her face with her sleeve. She needed some water—that and something else to eat, since she'd thrown her fruit at the trooper. She took the tooka cat out of her shirt. It sat quietly in the crook of her arm, resigned to its fate. Jyn stroked its head.

"I hope you're worth all this trouble, friend," she told the cat. "Let's find your owner, okay?"

Jyn wandered in and out of the stalls, pausing to buy another meiloorun and watching for the little girl. She ducked out of sight as she neared the sausage vendor, who was grumpily piling soaked coals back into his grill. He probably didn't want to see her again, even if he had helped her with that splash of oil.

Still cradling the cat, Jyn finished her fruit

and circled back to the teakettle stall where she'd first seen the little girl.

The child was still there, picking up the fallen teakettles and carefully stacking them on top of each other. The kettle vendor stood over her, hands on his hips.

"That's right, pick them all up," he said meanly. "There's one by the fabric stall, get that. Come on, girl, faster!"

The little girl fumbled a kettle, letting it fall with a clatter.

"Sorry," she whispered to the vendor, grabbing it.

The vendor threw his arms up in a *What's next?* gesture and stomped toward the back of his stall.

"Don't even think about leaving until they're all picked up," he shot over his shoulder.

Jyn paused a moment, watching the little girl work. The child sniffled quietly and hiccupped. Jyn couldn't wait another second. She stepped over to the girl.

"I think this is yours."

The little girl turned around. With a *mrrreoww*, the tooka cat leapt out of Jyn's arms—and straight into the girl's.

The little girl's face lit up with joy.

"Tookie! You're back!" she cried.

She hugged the creature to her chest. The cat's purring boomed like a motor. The little girl looked up at Jyn.

"You saved her. How did you do it? Who are you?"

Jyn swallowed hard and reached out to smooth back the girl's tangled black locks, but didn't say anything.

The little girl shifted the cat to her other arm and took Jyn's sweaty hand. Her little fingers looked very pale and smooth against Jyn's scarred, rough skin.

"You helped me. No one helps me."

Jyn shifted uncomfortably, not used to someone appreciating her, for anything. She didn't know what to say.

The little girl asked again, "Please, who are you?"

Finally Jyn knelt down and looked into the little girl's face.

"My name's Jyn Erso."

The little girl stared up at Jyn. Her eyes shone blue.

"Thank you, Jyn Erso."

A MESSAGE FROM MAZ:

It's almost time to go in, my friend. The moon has risen to its zenith. And we are almost out of wood. We've told many tales. And we have heard of heroes. Sometimes people who do small deeds can end up making a big difference. Look at all the flurrgs who have joined us. One . . . two . . . three . . . twenty in all. You never know when you're going to be a hero to someone.

Listen to all their croaking! What are they
saying? What's that? Oh! *I'm* your hero? Well,
that's very nice.

Throw this water on the fire, dear. I love
to hear the hiss. The white smoke will curl up
into the sky. The light and the warmth have
gone out. And it's time for us to go to bed.

ABOUT THE AUTHOR

EMMA CARLSON BERNE has written many books for children and young adults, including historical fiction, sports fiction, romances, and mysteries. She writes and runs after her three little boys in Cincinnati, Ohio.

LOOK FOR THESE BOOKS IN STORES NOW!

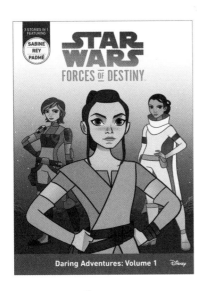